D1027810

For Sydney , mommy, Christina, Alexis, Chloe , Chasity, and Jasmine.

THE STRIKERS

WRITTEN BY GISELLE McCRAW

ILLUSTRATED BY CHASITY HAMPTON

CONTENTS

ACKNOWLEDGMENTS

I would like to thank my marvelous mother for being my editor. I would like to thank my terrific teacher Ashley Austin and Stephen Presti for encouraging me to actualize my full potential. When I didn't know I could do it, they knew I had it in me all along. My Grandma and Grandpa for always telling me to follow my dreams. My Aunt Janet who tells me to keep smiling and follow my passion. My Uncle who always tells me I am the Greatest Giselle and to put my best foot forward. My amazing illustrator for bringing my story to life. I would also like to thank my proofreader P. Lowe.

Chapter 1
FIRST PERIOD

Anyone would be surprised by the story that I'm about to tell you. It began with three girls named Lizbeth, Mia, and Giselle were all participants of the First Tee held at Mosholu golf course in the Bronx, NY. At this course there are nine holes hole 7 and Hole 9 being the longest. There is also a huge driving range where people can be found practicing their chipping and driving shots. Whenever a golfer hits a ball, on the range, it can be seen flying off into the distance. If it weren't for the ball truck that rides around the range retrieving those golf balls you'd never see them again. Adjacent to the first hole on the driving range stands a tall green shed where all the spare golf clubs are stored. Atop of the hill sits the Pro Shop and Sandwedge grill. The Sandwedge grill is famous for its delicious sandwiches. The best one is the Triple Decker bacon egg and avocado burger. They also serve shakes and other snacks. Next to the Sandwedge Grill is the clubhouse where all classes are held.

You can always smell the aroma of burgers being cooked while STEM (science, technology, engineering and math) class is in session. There is also the Pro Shop where they sell everything and anything you need to play golf. From golf shirts, to golf clubs, golf balls and hats. You see the thing about the game of golf is everthing is based on etiquette which means there is a specific rule for how to do just about everything.

It was a bright and sunny Monday and the greens on the golf course, near Banana Split Drive, were glistening because it had rained the night before. There were tons of tiny beads of water on the grass. It looked like the grounds keeper has polished each blade of grass individually. The sun was blazing and everyone thought the temperature felt like 100 degrees.

It was a happy day for almost everyone, except for one coach and her name was Coach Ally Weiss.

At golf camp the girls could always be seen with a smile on each and every one of their faces. Mia is a pretty, tall girl with a beige complexion. She is a little plump and she has long, dark brown hair. On the golf course Mia was always noticeable because of the way the soft wind blew against her hair making her hair swirl uncontrollably. Now Lizbeth is downright gorgeous. Her skin is golden beige with olive undertones. Her hair is wicked-witch black and wavy. She has a medium build and is average in height. Last but not least, is Giselle. Giselle has a reddish brown skin tone with curly, long wavy hair that would always shimmer and glimmer in the sun while her hair flowed effortlessly.

"Come on guys," Lizbeth shouted.

"Hey, wait up, you're going too fast," Mia hollered.

"Mia hurry up! We don't want to be late for first period," said Giselle.

"What do we have first period?" Mia questioned.

" Our first period is STEM!" Lizbeth and Giselle exclaimed in unison.

8

THUMPPP. Lizbeth **BLACKED OUT**, she had just been struck by a golf ball dead smack in the center of her forehead.

"Are you okay Lizbeth?" Giselle whispered in horror. Lizbeth didn't utter a word.

"Mia do you think she will wake up before 8:00?"

"I hope so because we have STEM in five minutes." There was a huge knot on Lizbeth's forehead and her cheeks were turning rosy red but she managed to keep it together. The girls quickly looked around for help but there was no one in sight. Mia and Giselle were tugging feverishly at Lizbeth's arms trying to lift her up. " UGGHHHH!" Giselle and Mia moaned.
They finally saw someone approaching them but could only make out the blonde flowing hair and a twig-like figure. As the figure

approached them they recognized her as their coach, Ally Weiss. "Ladies, why are we so loud, and why are we so late?" inquired Coach Weiss.

"Coach Weiss, Lizbeth was struck by a golf ball and we were trying to make sure she was ok", said Mia. We're headed to class now". said Giselle. They wave goodbye to coach Weiss and run to class.

Chapter 2
PEACH COBBLER

One Period Later...

"Come on, let's go back to the course! I want to practice my putting. At the last tournament I lost by one point. I'm certainly not going to let that happen again. That next tournament is mine." said Lizbeth with determination .

"Wait I have to go to the bathroom REALLY REALLY BADLY!" Mia cried as she hurried off. The bathroom was located in the back of the clubhouse next to the locker room. What's that smell? shrieked Giselle.

It smelled like a peachy drizzling goopy cobbler. Mia pushed the door to the bathroom open with huge force. **BAM**... The door slammed against the wall.

11

They saw someone standing in front of the sink drinking a concoction that smelled like a fruity peach cobbler.

"OH that's the peach cobbler I smelled," Giselle sniffed.

Coach Weiss ran into the bathroom stall slamming the door with a thunderous sound. Mia snuck into the stall next to Coach Weiss, stood on the toilet and peeked over the top while Giselle watched from underneath.

As they watched they saw a bright red ray of light appear from her eyes and mouth. They could see the light emanating through the door. Right before their very own eyes her skin was melting onto the floor in piles of peachy orange slime. Lizbeth had entered the bathroom and noticed the mysterious ray of light shining through the edges of the bathroom stall. They were all terrified and astonished. The three girls bolted from the bathroom in a tizzy and were flabbergasted by what they had just witnessed.

Once outside they really, really wanted to know what was going on so they huddled by the lockers. As they waited for the time to pass, they told stories of what they thought Coach Weiss could be doing in the bathroom. "Maybe she's taking an evil witch potion to make her strong", said Giselle. Maybe she took some old medication said Mia. Maybe she's doing drugs. I've seen commercials about what drugs can to do people, said Lizbeth. Finally Coach Weiss came out and she looked drastically different than she'd ever looked before. Her eyes were a fiery red and her lips were black. Her body frame was so skinny. All you could see was bones. She was a living skeleton. She was now wearing a thin black cloak that hung loosely off of her bony neck. "She's ugly!" Mia shrieked.

"Isn't she the world's worst villain?" Lizbeth exclaimed. Lizbeth remembered seeing a picture of her on the cover of World's Worst Villain magazine. In the article she read that the villain was planning to destroy the world and the first phase of her plan was to destroy all of the golf courses. She was going to secretly plant a black root that would spread across the course and destroy the greens in nanoseconds. According to the article the Villain was on the loose and hadn't been seen in months. The girls gasped.

They couldn't stand
the idea of Villain
Weiss harming anyone
else because they knew she
wanted to rule the world, so
they decided to hatch a plan.
"I think we should call the police
to take her to villain jail," Lizbeth
said.
"No we should gather a super
group and call them The
Strikers!" Giselle exclaimed.
"I think we should try to get
her in the shed and lock her
in there," Mia said.
"I agree with Giselle,"
Lizbeth whispered.
"So it looks like
we're going
with

Giselle's idea," They all said.

"Yes, but first we have to find out what is a blackroot!", Giselle asserted. As the girls headed off to the clubhouse to research the blackroot, they had no clue Coach Weiss had overheard their entire conversation.

Back at the clubhouse the girls quickly sat down and logged onto their tablets. They knew they had a limited amount of time to find out about the blackroot, so they immediately began to Google it. Lizbeth shouted, "I found it". A blackroot is derived from the skin of a rare snake that is venomous. When dipped into a blackweed ink and planted inside of a divot it becomes a toxic liquid contaminating any and everything it comes in contact with but it has a smell resembling peach cobbler. It takes 48 hours to destroy 9 holes. "Oh my gosh"

screamed Mia. "We probably don't have got much time left", said Giselle. "We've got to stop villain Weiss from planting the blackroot", said Lizabeth. "How do we know she hasn't already planted it", shrieked Mia. Well we have to find out, said Giselle. The girls decide to head over to Lizbeth's castle where they can have something to eat and figure out what will be their next move.

Chapter 3
THE TRANSFORMATION

While walking to the castle something unexpected happened. The wooden ramp over the moat that connects the grounds to the castle doors suddenly gave way and the girls plunged into the water below. It's freezing in here yelled, Lizbeth. Then suddenly to their surprise the color of the water turned aquamarine. It felt refreshing but bone-chilling cold. The water started to glow and out of the beautiful aquamarine water came each girl donning superhero outfits. First, Loyal Lizbeth appeared wearing a long cape with red and yellow stripes. Her boots were a fiery red with shiny buckles. It was a very shiny suit with glossy sparkles all over it. Next appeared Marvelous Mia in a superhero suit that had purple, pink, blue stars and hearts.

It was ridiculously bright and rockstar shiny.
And finally, Greatest Giselle stood confident
and tall wearing a gold, teal, and white, glow
in the dark glamorously sparkly superhero

suit. She looked like a member of the royal family.

With the ramp damaged, Lizbeth says, "let's go to back of the castle, there is another entryway. The girls quickly followed behind Lizbeth to the back entrance. Once inside the castle they dashed up the stairs to Loyal Lizbeth's room.

In their confusion they each looked at the reflection of their new appearance. Wow, Isabella utters, look at us. We look so beautiful says Giselle. So, after a moment of pause and reflection, Lizbeth shouts I'm starving. The girls head down to the kitchen where Lizbeth's mom, Ashley is preparing dinner. Hi girls! Are you playing dress up again? Uh...yes we are. We are trying on some new dresses from Giselle's closet, Lizbeth responded.

"Oh great, well are you hungry?", asked Ashley. "Yes we surely are!" they said in unison. Well I made spaghetti and meatballs for dinner and for dessert we've got banana pudding", said Lizbeth's mom. They all sat down at the neatly set long leafed wooden table and Lizbeth's mom served all the girls. While the girls ate dinner they got to talking about Villain Weiss. "I think we might need a few more girls to help us with Weiss", said Giselle . "You got that right. Maybe we can recruit a few more girls from the community", said Mia. "Why don't we have something with an Escape the room theme here in the castle. We can invite a few girls and see who escapes in the fastest time . Then those girls will be invited to join the Strikers.", declared Lizbeth.

After dessert the girls head back to Lizbeth's room where they got to work sending out email invitations to girls they know in the community.

Chapter 4
THE STRIKERS

Over the course of the next 3 days they receive responses from 12 girls. They took care of all the details, to make sure the event went off without a hitch. Giselle researched what types of things were in Escape Rooms, bought a countdown clock and bought all sorts of gadgets. That Thursday all 12 girls showed up to the castle to participate in "Escape the Room" The invitees went into the Escape room in groups of four. The girls with the fastest time were Isabella, Stoney and Peyton. Mia congratulated the girls on their achievement and then gave a nod to Giselle. Did you all have fun ?, asked Isabella. I love escape the room", chimed Stoney. Yeah it was awesome , said Peyton.

Well the reason we put this together is because we are forming a group, but not just any group. We're called the Strikers. We need a group that will be mentally and physically strong and by you completing this task we know you will make perfect additions to the group. Now that you are accepted into the group we can tell you everything, said Giselle. Peyton, Isabella and Stoney exclaimed, "I'm in". Loyal Lizbeth sat all the girls down and told them EVERYTHING. The new girls looked a bit terrified but excited and up for the challenge. Giselle, Lizbeth and Mia led the 3 new girls down to the same broken ramp where they had gained their newfound outfits. All at once, they pushed the new girls into the moat.

Smart Stoney first came out of the water with her smooth chocolate complexion with dark chocolate braids in the form of a crown. She wore an orange and yellow neon suit. Then, appeared Peyton. She wore a red and white glow in the dark dress, to go with her beige flawless skin. Her hair was straight and she actually kind of looked like Giselle. Lastly, Incredible Isabella rounded out the group. She was dressed in a neon green bright superhero suit. Her hair was mocha brown and her beige skin was as smooth as silk. Now the new group members were checking each other out from head to toe. Still none of the girls had any idea there was so much more than just their new found beautiful appearance. "With Great Power Comes Great Responsibility," once a superhero quoted. They were soon going to learn what that actually meant.

WE ARE THE STRIKERS,

Incredible Isabella, Greatest Giselle, Marvelous Mia, Powerful Payton, Loyal Lizbeth and Smart Stoney.

Chapter 5
SUPERPOWERS

Things had not been the same for the girls since the incident at the castle moat. The girls had all started feeling different so they agreed to meet up that day at Greatest Giselle's house at 3pm. Earlier that day Giselle had been talking to a friend on the phone when her mom knocked on the door and reminded Giselle to clean up her room. Giselle muttered to herself, " I wish this room would clean itself up. " With her very own eyes she began to witness everything in the room moving to its proper place. Startled, Giselle fell into a pile of clothes. She would of fell on the ground if it weren't for the clothes. "Thanks clothes! Thanks Powers! Wait!, I have powers?" Giselle starts jumping and twirling around the room , bumping into the dresser and accidentally knocking over and breaking a few golf trophies. "Oh No, my trophies!" Giselle says while becoming saddened. She began to wail. Wait, I have powers I can fix these trophies. She wished that the trophies were fixed and as they began to come back together she shouted, "**WOOHOO**!" Giselle starts thinking about what else to add to her wishlist. I could buy mommy a new diamond necklace, I could get a car, live in a mansion. I could even help the homeless. Her mom hears all the commotion and knocks on the door again. "Giselle! Giselle! Is everything alright? Are you almost finished? " Yes mom, almost done. Her mom opens the door and says "how did you clean your room so fast?"

Oh I only had a few things to put away, said Giselle. Then Giselle says to herself, mommy will never have to buy anything again. She began doing this over and over again, wishing for headbands, books, toys and slime. Every single one of the wishes she made came true. Just then she realized she had wish granting superpowers. Giselle whispered to herself, "I have to tell someone! "Wait, why aren't they here yet, it's 3:30pm? I wish they would get here right now". Shortly thereafter, the doorbell rang, Ding Dong, Ding Dong. It was the Strikers. Giselle ran to greet the girls at the door. "What took you so long? I thought you'd never get here," said Giselle. She then led them up the stairs into her meticulously cleaned bedroom.

All at once the girls began to share their

experiences with each other. Everyone was talking over one another so you could hardly hear what anyone was saying. "I can't hear anyone, I wish they would stop talking". In an effort to get everyone's attention Giselle switched off the lights. The room became eerily quiet. She quickly turned the lights back on and saw that all the girls mouths were frozen shut and their eyes were bulging out of their head. The room was deafeningly quiet. She was frantic. "Uh-oh', Giselle said. "Wait, I can unfreeze them, she thought. "I hope this works. I wish everyone would talk one at a time and listen to each other. They all looked at each other and were astonished. "Listen up here!", Giselle said firmly. "There have been some strange things going on and I'm not so sure how to explain them". One by one, the girls started to share their now awkward life experiences. They all discovered what powers they possessed. Loyal Lizbeth was able to read minds. Marvelous Mia could shrink and enlarge people or things. Powerful Peyton was strong like Popeye. Smart Stoney was beyond intelligent. She could figure out anything. Incredible Isabella possessed speed greater than a cheetah. Together they felt undefeatable.

Back at the golf course Coach Weiss was standing outside of the locker room. She had become quite concerned about what the girls might have seen in the bathroom. "I need to find out if anyone is on my trail, especially the EVP, Extreme Villain Police. These meddling girls could ruin my vicious plan to use the blackroot to destroy the golf courses and kill everyone in this terrible pathetic world!" Weiss exclaimed.

HaHaHaHa!!" Weiss laughed.

Coach Weiss hurried off from the locker room to hole number 6 on the golf course. She grabbed her 9 iron, hit the shot and scored an eagle . As Coach Weiss scanned her finger on the flag at hole number 6 a mysterious entrance to her lair opened. She slid down the pole slowly, with her feet hitting the ground with a THUD and her villain league appeared out of the darkness. There were dozens of villains chanting , "Weiss rules, Weiss rules". She smiled a wicked smile and laughed as she lifted her arm straight up into the air and said, "I shall not stop until the world is mine, under my rules!" Weiss hollered at everyone in her villain league. "Muah HaHaHaHa!

Meanwhile back in Giselle's bedroom, the girls were discussing their powers and how

they could use their powers to defeat
the Villain "We have to somehow, as
superheroes, challenge Weiss and defeat her
and her cruel villain league! We can't let her
get that blackroot near the divot. " Giselle
exclaimed with confidence. A few minutes
later Smart Stoney typed up a note to send to
Villain Weiss.

Chapter 6
THE NOTE

The next morning when Coach Weiss arrived at the golf course, she noticed an email from a sender she did not recognize. When she opened it up it, it said "The Strikers" and it read:

Friday, June 19th,
Zip Code 10457

" We know who you are. Your reign of terror is over. If you are really a villain, come to Banana Split Drive tonight at 8:00pm and show us what you have. If you indeed want to rule the world, as it exist, you must first get past us.

Good Luck,
The Strikers

"Well!!!! If they want us they can have us," Weiss challenged.
She was so annoyed, that she quickly drafted a reply back stating:

Dear Worthless Strikers,

If you really want us, have us! You know you'll lose so what's the whole point of wasting my time fighting you. I'd rather see someone dance and puke than see your face, Strikers. See you in your loss. Oh and we'll be there, just wait! You better watch yourself. Time is ticking! Remember I'm the coach, I'm still in charge here!

Regards,
Weiss and the Villain league

Chapter 7
BANANA SPLIT DRIVE

At 8pm sharp, that evening the Strikers had shown up to Banana Split Drive. They noticed a small figured person wearing a dark red cloak with VL in BIG BOLD BLACK letters. Lizbeth immediately asks , "who's thaaaaaat"? "Oh it's my new assistant, Sydney." Weiss responded.

"Respect me because I can harm you with the snap of a finger because I do not play with little kitties!" Sassy Sydney exclaimed. Incredible Isabella charges at Sassy Sydney with lightning speed but then realizes she does not know what to do with this speed. She starts running around in circles nonstop. Greatest Giselle then makes a wish for Weiss to trip over the rock but realizes nothing happens. Then Greatest Giselle sets out to attack Weiss but she trips over the same rock she meant for Weiss to trip over. It is in that moment Giselle realizes that she can only use her wishes for good. If she makes a bad wish she will suffer all the consequences of that ill intended wish. Suddenly Powerful Peyton tries to move the rock Giselle tripped over from underneath her but when she picks it up she accidentally crushes it because she doesn't know her own strength. Loyal Lizbeth is reading everyone's minds but doesn't know how to process all the thoughts. She just watches while being speechless and still as a statue. Smart Stoney watches from the sideline and feels helpless because she doesn't have an active power and the power she does have she doesn't know how to use.

" Guys I don't know what to do, what should I do what should do?" All the girls are too busy trying to win the fight individually using their new found powers, instead of acting as a real team, thought Smart Stoney.

BAM! BAM! WHACK! SLAM! HIT! POW! SLAM! SLASH!

Who knows who won the battle? Losers! Muah Ha Ha Ha Ha. Oh and if you were paying attention you would know whose laugh that is, the laugh is Villain Weiss's laugh so that means that the villain league won, unfortunately.

It was dark and cold as the Strikers ran sluggishly back to Giselle's house. They had a difficult time finding their way through the bushes and woods along Banana Split Drive. When they finally arrived the girls were shivering. They were emotionally and physically defeated. The girls knew they needed to regroup. They couldn't let things end this way. "I don't know how we lost but we are going to fight again", Loyal Lizbeth exclaimed.

"We need a well thought out plan", Smart Stoney," whispered. Let's work together this time to use our powers for good to save the world. We need to figure out who uses what powers and when. "Great idea!" Powerful Peyton shouted.

"Let's do it!" everyone shouted in unison! "We demand a rematch!" And if we perish, WE PERISH!", Greatest Giselle exclaimed.

They sent a second letter to Weiss and her villains inviting them to a rematch, with the hopes they would win and spread kindness throughout the world while protecting the golf course from Villain Weiss and her minions.

The next morning this letter was delivered to Weiss:

We demand a rematch! If you're really villains, come and fight us again. Let's see who is the real ruler of this world . Same place, same time, back to Banana Split Drive .

Chapter 8
REMATCH

When everyone arrived back at the battleground all you could see were the glowing lights and dark figures in all shapes and sizes. As the Strikers approached they saw Villain Weiss with her hands on her hips firmly planted into the concrete. It was time to put the plan into action. The Strikers linked arms and without delay Greatest Giselle made a wish. "I wish the Strikers would all work together and use our powers to defeat Weiss and her villians successfully. Loyal Lizbeth began to read the minds of Weiss and her villains telling the other Strikers what Weiss was secretly plotting next. Without hesitation, Incredible Isabella released her arms from the link and circled around the villains and Weiss with lightning speed to create a vacuum that lifted them up and suspended them in the air.

Greatest Giselle quickly wished for a cage to imprison the villains, but it landed in the wrong spot. Powerful Peyton saw that it was in the wrong spot and then lifted up the titanium cage and with great might moved it to where the villains would fall into it. Marvelous Mia shrunk the villains and Weiss and then Giselle wished for them to be trapped inside the cage for good. Weiss and the villains screeched as they were shrunk. Ahhhhhhhhhh! Smart Stoney realized now that the villains had been shrunk they could escape, so she quickly told Giselle to wish for a jar. Giselle made the wish and transported Weiss and her villains into the jar.

"We did it guys!" they all shouted in unison! "We make the best team there could ever be!" Peyton squealed. "We saved the glorious world from those villains!"

"Nooooooooooooooooooooooooo!" Isabella exclaimed, as the lid of the jar twisted and turned, rolling on the floor , eventually opening. The villains scurried away setting out to make a potion to return them to their normal size.

"You didn't think this would be the end of the story did you?"

"Because it's not," Villain Weiss exclaimed in a chipmunk voice.

"Bzzzzzzzzzzzzzzzzzzzzzz!" A bee came right over and stung the villains and villain Weiss.

BZZZZZZZZZZZZZZZZZZZZZZ again!

Chapter 9
HOORAYS

That evening the girls walked to Lizbeth's castle. Lizbeth's mom, Ashley invited everyone into the kingdom to celebrate the victory over the villains " Everyone lets please praise the Strikers for getting rid of the villains" Ashley exclaimed. She turned the microphone over to Loyal Lizbeth as Greatest Giselle, Incredible Isabella, Marvelous Mia and Powerful Peyton stood side by side holding hands. The crowd cheered with glee. Us girls are powerful and unique together. Our newfound powers were only one part of our strength. We needed to use our unique talents to devise a plan for good. We thought and fought successfully!

They all ate juicy chicken, pizza and peach cobbler. "Thanks mom for the food, " Loyal Lizbeth said pleasantly.

Suddenly the door slightly opened and they noticed a yellow jacket bee. Riding on the bee was tiny Weiss. Everyone shouted as they tried to swat it but missed. It was then The Strikers learned With Great Power Comes Great Responsibility's BBBBBBBB BBBBBBBBBBBBBBBBBBBBBBBBZ ZZZ ZZZZZZ ZZZZZ ZZZ ZZZZZZZZZ ZZZZZ ZZZ ZZZZZ ZZZZZZZZ ZZZZZZZZZZ ZZZZZ ZZZZZZZZ

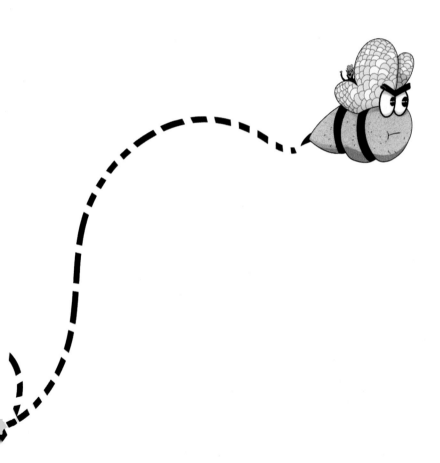